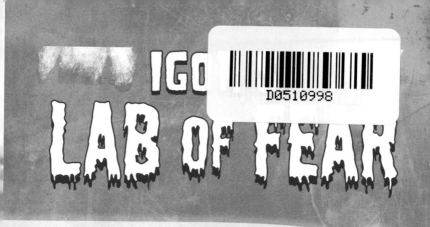

IGOR'S LAB OF FEAR

BRAIN INVADERS

by Michael Dahl   illustrated by Andy Catling

Raintree is an imprint of Capstone Global Library Limited, a company
incorporated in England and Wales having its registered office at
264 Banbury Road, Oxford, OX2 7DY – Registered company number:
6695582

www.raintree.co.uk
myorders@raintree.co.uk

Text © Capstone Global Library Limited 2017
The moral rights of the proprietor have been asserted.

ISBN 978-1-4747-2532-3 (paperback)
20 19 18 17 16
10 9 8 7 6 5 4 3 2 1

British Library Cataloguing in Publication Data
A full catalogue record for this book is available from the British
Library.

COVER ILLUS...
DESIGNER: K...
EDITORS: Se...

Printed in China

CONTENTS

Greetings, my friend!

How did you know
I'd be down here?

Oh, you just followed
the noise. And the
slimy footprints.

Well, that's using
your head. He-he.

Yes, I've been very busy down here. I've been looking through my special collection.

What's that, you ask? Is that a brain behind the glass?

It does look like a brain, doesn't it?

Pull up a chair. I'm going to tell you a story...

CHAPTER ONE
PURPLE RAIN

Diego and Martin looked up at the sky.

They had never seen such strange clouds.

"That one is purple," Diego shouted.

"I bet there will be lightning," Martin said.

A spear of lightning **FLASHED** across the sky.

The rain fell harder.

The two friends ran out of the ocean.
They jogged up the beach.

They hid under a tree.

Martin sighed. "No more swimming today," he said.

The boys had skipped school.

That morning, they had caught a
bus. They got off at the forest.

They had walked through the
forest. Soon they reached the ocean.

They had planned to spend the whole day there. They would swim. They would surf. They would snorkel.

But now it was raining. Their plans were <u>ruined</u>.

Diego pointed at the sky. "Even the lightning is purple," he said.

Then other STRANGE lights appeared in the sky. They blinked like stars in the clouds.

The lights reminded Martin of cameras flashing.

Diego poked Martin. "Maybe it's a **UFO**," he joked.

Martin rolled his eyes.

The weird storm didn't last long.
Soon the waves calmed down.

The clouds changed from purple to grey.

A cool breeze blew off the sea.

Martin shivered.

"Look!" Diego said. "Someone is out there."

CHAPTER TWO
SURVIVORS

A fishing boat was drifting in the ocean.

The waves pushed the boat towards shore. It looked empty.

"Hello!" the boys called out.

No one answered.

Then the boat got stuck in the shallow water.

The waves slapped against it. It rocked back and forth.

Diego and Martin ran back into the water.

They swam out to the boat. They climbed into it.

It was not empty. Five men and two women lay in the boat.

<u>None</u> of them were moving.

One man still held a fishing pole.

One of the women had a small dog in her lap. It sat like a lump of hair and did not move.

"What happened to them?" Diego whispered.

"Let's leave," Martin said. "<u>Now!</u>"

"They don't look sick," said Diego.

One of the men started to **GURGLE**.

The boys jumped back.

They saw the man's face tremble.

Something was **COMING** out of his mouth.

CHAPTER THREE
JELLYFISH

The boys leaped off the boat.

SPLASH!

Martin pointed at the water. "Look out!" he shouted. "Jellyfish!"

Diego looked down. A swarm of jellyfish circled him.

Touching a jellyfish is dangerous. Their long, wavy tentacles carry POISON.

Diego and Martin swam as fast as they could.

A few feet from the shore, the ocean water began to swirl.

The waves grew larger and larger around them.

Jellyfish were everywhere.

Diego ran onto the beach.

He plopped down on the sand. He caught his breath.

Martin was gone. "Where are you?!" Diego yelled.

"*ARRRRGGGGHHH!*" someone moaned.

Diego glanced around. "Martin?" he said. "Is that you?"

Then he saw the boat. The gurgling man was standing up now.

"**ARRRRGGGGHHH!**" the man moaned.

The sunlight was in Diego's eyes. It was hard to see.

What's wrong with his head? Diego wondered.

Something large was crawling out of the man's mouth.

It looked like a jellyfish.

It **WRIGGLED** out of the man's mouth. Then it sat on top of the man's head.

The creature looked like a brain. A brain with spider legs.

The other passengers in the boat stood up. Diego watched, frozen with fear.

All of them were moaning.

All of them had jellyfish brains crawling out of their mouths.

And they were staring right at Diego.

CHAPTER FOUR
BRAINS?

The creatures started walking onto the beach.

Diego stood still. His feet felt like concrete in the sand.

Jellyfish were walking up the beach. They were headed right for him.

Their long tentacles carried them across the sand.

They waved their tentacles in the air. The brains throbbed like beating hearts.

Diego could see them **PUFF** up like balloons and then grow smaller.

It looked like they were breathing.

Splashing sounds caught the boy's attention.

The people on the boat were swimming towards shore.

Diego turned. Diego ran.

He darted across the sand. He entered the forest.

The jellyfish brains were slow. But they kept coming.

Diego heard a gurgling sound behind him.

He stopped and turned around.

A creature stepped out from behind a bush. Then <u>another</u> stepped out, too.

The creatures clicked their tentacles together.

How many are there? Diego asked himself. *Where did they come from?!*

Then the boy saw a shadow next to a tree.

Diego's eyes fixed on the shadow. It wasn't a shadow at all.

It was Martin!

Diego ran to his friend's side.

"We've got to get out of here," Diego said. "These freaks are everywhere!"

Martin slowly and quietly turned his head. A long skinny tentacle poked out of his mouth.

Skipping school can be risky.

I'm sure Diego and Martin only planned to spend one day at the beach. But they never showed up to school again.

I was so worried about those poor boys. So I spoke with their teachers.

They said the two boys got into trouble all the time.

"They just didn't use their brains," one of their teachers said.

Well, it looks like someone else is using them now!

He-he. Heh Heh Heh Heh

PROFESSOR IGOR'S LAB NOTES

Why might a jellyfish want to steal a person's brain? Because it has no brain of its own!

Instead of a brain, a jellyfish uses a system of nerves. The nerves help it know when to move and eat.

A jellyfish also doesn't have any bones. Its soft, squishy body is called a bell. Under the bell is a mouth.

A jellyfish's long tentacles catch its food. Prey such as fish, shrimp, or other jellyfish get tangled up in the tentacles. The tentacles sting the prey. They release poison into the prey. The prey is paralysed. It can't move. Then the tentacles slowly move the prey into the jellyfish's mouth. My, what a delicious feast!

Jellyfish stings can be painful, even deadly, to humans. Be careful when swimming in water known to have jellyfish. And be extra careful they don't get to your brain!

GLOSSARY

GURGLE to make a low, bubbling sound in the throat

NERVE a thin strand in the body that carries messages

PARALYSE to make someone or something unable to move

PREY an animal hunted by another animal for food

PUFF to swell or become filled with air

SNORKEL to swim underwater with a special tube for breathing

TENTACLE a long, armlike body part some animals use to touch, grab, or smell

THROB to beat hard or fast

TREMBLE to shake or shiver uncontrollably

UFO an object in the sky thought to be a spaceship from another planet; UFO is short for Unidentified Flying Object.

DISCUSSION QUESTIONS

1. Was the bad weather a sign that something bad was about to happen? Explain why or why not.

2. What do you think happened to the people on the boat? How come none of them were moving?

3. Why was it a bad idea for Martin and Diego to go to the beach that day? Do you think they got what they deserved in the end? Explain why or why not.

WRITING PROMPTS

1. Imagine you were a brain-stealing jellyfish. Explain why you might want to steal a human's brain. Write about how you might benefit.

2. How would you fight off a brain-stealing jellyfish? Maybe you would need some special powers. Write about how you would protect yourself.

3. What happens next in this story? You decide! Write a chapter about what happens after Diego sees Martin with a tentacle sticking out of his mouth.

AUTHOR BIOGRAPHY

Michael Dahl, the author of the Library of Doom, Dragonblood, and Troll Hunters series, has a long list of things he's afraid of: dark rooms, small rooms, damp rooms (all of which describe his writing area), storms, rabid squirrels, wet paper, raisins, flying in planes (especially taking off, cruising, and landing), and creepy dolls. He hopes that by writing about fear he will eventually be able to overcome his own. So far it isn't working. But he is afraid to stop, so he continues to write. He lives in a haunted house in Minneapolis, Minnesota.

ILLUSTRATOR BIOGRAPHY

Andy Catling is a professional scribbler and splurger of pictures who has illustrated for publishers around the world. Andy works in traditional mediums and digital wot-nots using a rigorous mangle-like process. First he draws a picture. Then he rubs it out and draws it again. He colours using watercolour, pencils, and ink, sniffs it, screws it up, and starts over. The digital work process is much the same but without the sniffing. (All digital artwork smells of screen wipe.) Andy lives in the United Kingdom. He thinks he is a pirate.